On the edge of the jungle, where the herbivores grazed,
four little dinosaurs spent their days
playing in the Cretaceous sun,
following tracks and having fun.

With teeth as long
as you are tall,
he'd soon make a snack
of one so small.

His feet go STOMP!
His jaws go CRUNCH!
In the blink of an eye
you'd be his LUNCH!

Bonehead, Tiny,
Fin and Bill
went off to play
up on the hill.
The Gigantosaurus
was on their minds
till Bonehead said:

THUD
THUD
THUD

They ran!
They hid!
They shook with fear!
The GIGANTOSAURUS
was coming near!

"But you passed
my Emergency Warning Trial.
Now I think I'll keep watch
from that rock awhile."

BOM BOM BOM BOM

They ran! They hid!
They shook with fear!

The GIGANTOSAURUS
was coming near!

But there was no STOMP.
There was no CRUNCH.
No hungry beast after snacks to munch...

"It's old DIPLODOCUS!"
Bonehead laughed.

"You ran! You hid!
You're all so daft!"

"But danger lurks,
as you need to learn.
I'll look out from that
enormous fern."

THUMP THUMP THUMP

They **RAN!** They **HID!**
They shook with fear!
The GIGANTOSAURUS
was coming near!

But there was no STOMP.
There was no CRUNCH.
No carnivore with a
whiff of lunch...

"It's STEGOSAURUS!"
Bonehead laughed.
"You ran! You hid!
You're all so DAFT!"

"But at least
you've passed my final test.
Now I'm going for a nap
in that comfy nest."

Then, seconds later,
the cry began...

GIGANTOSAURUS!
Run as fast as you can!

But though his friends heard
what Bonehead cried,
by now they knew
that Bonehead lied.

"That's it!" said Bill.
"We're off to explore.
And we're not going to
play with YOU
ANYMORE."

No one left to trick, Bonehead was alone.

He began to wish he was back home.

For an awful noise was coming near,

and now there WAS good reason for fear...

The feet went

STOMP!

And though Bonehead thought they'd run in fright,
his friends just shrugged and said,
"Yeah, right!"

MEET THE DINOSAURS IN THIS BOOK...

PARASAUROLOPHUS
Palaeontologists* think this dinosaur's large crest was used to make sounds!

TRICERATOPS
This dinosaur had a huge skull – 1/3 the length of its whole body.

ANKYLOSAURUS
A full-grown adult weighed as much as 5 or 6 tonnes!

STEGOSAURUS
This dinosaur's spiked tail is called a thagomizer.

*Palaeontologist: a scientist who studies prehistoric times.

BRACHIOSAURUS
A truly huge herbivore, Tiny's mum will grow to be even bigger than Diplodocus!

DIPLODOCUS
This giant dinosaur had a comically tiny brain.

PTERODACTYL
There's no such thing as a pterodactyl, but that's what most people call pterosaurs (flying lizards). What Bonehead meant to say was pteranodon, or more specifically quetzalcoatlus, but he couldn't pronounce that.

GIGANTOSAURUS
This scary dinosaur was made up for this book!*